Library of Congress Cataloging-in-Publication Data

Rinck, Maranke.
[Prinsenkind. English]
The prince child / Maranke Rinck ; illustrations by Martijn van der Linden.—1st U.S. ed.
p. cm.
Summary: Musing about the young frog prince's party and the gifts they bear, various animals head for the celebration.
ISBN 1-932425-15-2 (alk. paper)
[1. Gifts—Fiction. 2. Parties—Fiction. 3. Animals—Fiction.] I. Linden, Martijn van der, ill. II. Title.

PZ7.R464Pr 2004
[E]-dc22   2004046930

The Prince Child

Maranke Rinck

ILLUSTRATIONS BY

Martijn van der Linden

Front Street & Lemniscaat

Soon

It's almost time for the party.

Sun lights up the valley and makes the water sparkle.

Soon animals from everywhere will come to this place to celebrate.

Right now they are getting ready.

Far away, the heron swings his cap up onto his head. The lizard races across sticks and stones. High in the mountains the snow cat pads along, no time to dilly-dally.

Soon many animals will be here for the party with their presents.

THE HERON

"A song," says the heron. "That's what my gift will be." He practices his clicks and quacks.

The grass sighs.

"What is it?" asks the heron.

"What kind of song is that?" says the grass.

"You don't think it's pretty?" asks the heron.

"Oh, well," says the grass. "I'm just grass. What do I know?"

The heron is silent for a moment.

"A song is made from sounds that come from the heart."

"Is that so?" asks the grass.

"Absolutely," says the heron, nodding.

"Then sing," says the grass.

So the heron continues on his way, singing.

THE SNOW CAT

"Look at me."

The snow cat looks around.

"Look at me," she hears again.

Suddenly she sees a little crystal ball, almost invisible in the snow. It rolls closer and closer and stops at her feet.

"Take me with you," says the little ball. "I'll show you the way."

"With pleasure," whispers the snow cat.

"But when we get there, you must promise to give me away," says the little ball.

The snow cat promises.

THE LIZARD

"Wait a minute!" the lizard calls out. "Not so fast!"
His friend is racing far ahead of him, her tail all a-wiggle.
"Hey!" he shouts. She doesn't look back.

A broken stick is lying across the path. The lizard scrabbles across. He almost tumbles off. "Have you got our gift?" he calls out.

"Yes," she answers him. "We'll give it together," she cries out from far ahead.

He sighs with relief and walks on, at his own speed. They will make it to the party, and give their gift together.

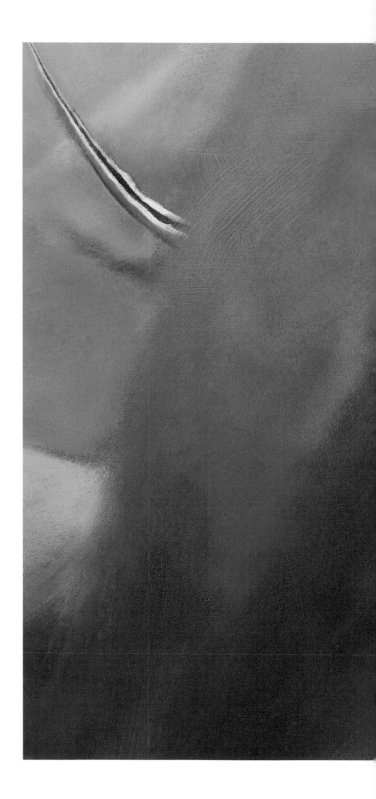

THE CRANE

With great care, the crane puts one foot in front of the other. She pretends she is balancing a book on her head, and tells herself that she cannot let it fall. Tall and upright, she proceeds.

This is how I will make my entrance, she says to herself. This is how I will present my gift.

With downcast eyes she places one of her most beautiful feathers on the ground in front of her and practices saying, "Please accept my humble offering."

Yes, I am ready, she says to herself, ready for the celebration.

THE GERBIL

Do I look all right? Are the flowers the perfect touch?

The gerbil found the flowers, the color of the sun, growing in the sand.
Many creatures had tried to pick them, but they would not let themselves be
picked.
  "Do you think," the gerbil asked, "that I might have a try?"
  The others laughed at him. They said, "All right, little fellow, you go ahead."
  The gerbil walked across the sand. He pressed his cheek against the stem.
  "Dear flowers," he whispered, "may I bring you to the party?"

Now he is ready.

The Marabou

"Let's all concentrate," says the marabou.

For a long time no one says a word.

"Ready?" asks the marabou.

"Yes, yes," mutter his friends. "Yes, quite ready."

"Good," says the marabou. "Here we go." He squats down and sticks out his wings like a ramp, and one by one his friends climb up, higher and higher, one atop the other. They form a tower.

"One, two, three..." shouts the marabou.

The tower starts to sway.

"Hoorah! Hoorah! Hoorah!" they all shout together. Then they fall to the ground, rubbing their knees and smoothing out their feathers.

"That's quite enough practice, I should think," says the marabou.

"Yes," say his friends. "Time to get going."

THE BEAVER

The beaver sails along, pushing his present in front of him.

"I'm going to a party," he shouts. "A party for a prince!"

The water washes aside twigs and leaves so he can freely pass.

After a while the beaver shouts again, "A party. A princely party!"

The water gives him a little push from behind.

This is great, the beaver says to himself. All I have to do is float.

A few minutes later he comes to a stop.

"Come on there, water," he says. "Give me some help."

The current grows strong and pushes him hard. Twigs hang from the beaver's fur. Dirty leaves slap against his nose. He almost loses his gift in the water.

"How's that?" asks the water.

"Sorry," says the beaver. "Sorry. For a moment I forgot who I was talking to."

The water calms down. The beaver swims on.

"We're going to a party," he shouts. "The water and I, together. A princely party!"

The Monkey

The monkey is resting but her eyes are open. She is dreaming of the party. She is wondering, will the prince be handsome?

She rolls over on her side.

She would like to be a princess.

"Princess Monkey," she giggles. She sits up and begins braiding a crown of daisies. "And this will be my crown."

She puts the crown on top of her cap. She feels like a princess already.

THE MARTEN

"And you," ask the chickadees. "What are you giving?"
"I'm giving poetry," the marten says solemnly.
The chickadees chirp loudly all at once. "What's that?" they want to know.
The marten clears his throat. "O..." he begins.
"Yes?" they ask.
"No. 'O' is how it starts," says the marten.
"Oh," say the chickadees.
"Right," says the marten. "Then it goes like this:

O you are like an olive,
So green and oh so small.
Later when you've become a king
You'll probably be tall.

"There," says the marten. "That's poetry."
The chickadees twitter. "We're giving a peanut necklace," they say. "Will that be all right, do you think?"
"Certainly," says the marten. "That's nice, too."

The Hyena

The hyena is watching.

"Look how many there are…," he whispers.

More animals than he has ever seen.

He watches them greet each other and gather around the water. He sees what presents they have brought.

The hyena is going to give his amulet—the amulet whose good luck has blessed his journey to the party.

A shout rises from near the water. "Hoorah! Hoorah! Hoorah for the young prince!"

The hyena can wait no longer. It is time to join the celebration.

THE YOUNG PRINCE

Alone, on a lily pad, sits the young prince.
He is wearing a tiny gold crown.

The party has begun. Everyone is waving
and cheering. They have all brought presents:
songs, poetry, flowers, a crystal ball.

Has anyone brought what the prince wants
most? Has anyone brought him a kiss?

It is time to make his wish.